EARTH'S NATURAL BIOMES

FOREST BIOMES

Louise and Richard Spilsbury

WAYLAND
www.waylandbooks.co.uk

First published in Great Britain in 2017 by Wayland

Copyright © Wayland, 2017

Editor: Hayley Fairhead
Design: Smart Design Studio
Map (page 9) by Stefan Chabluk

ISBN: 978 1 5263 0122 2
10 9 8 7 6 5 4 3 2 1

MIX
Paper from
responsible sources
FSC® C104740
FSC
www.fsc.org

Wayland, an imprint of
Hachette Children's Group
Part of Hodder and Stoughton
Carmelite House
50 Victoria Embankment
London EC4Y 0DZ

An Hachette UK Company
www.hachette.co.uk
www.hachettechildrens.co.uk

Printed and bound in China

All photographs except where mentioned supplied by
Nature Picture Library www.naturepl.com
Front cover(main), p5 and p32 Klein & Hubert; title page(main) and p6 David Norton; p4 Floris
van Breugel; imprint page(b) and p7 Luis Quinta; title page(b) and p8 John Abbott; contents page(t)
and p9 main Nick Garbutt; back cover(l), title page(t) and p10 Jussi Murtosaari; p11 Eric Baccega;
back cover(r) and p12 Luiz Claudio Marigo; front cover(b), imprint page(t) and p13 Mark Bowler; p14
Chris Mattison; p15 and p31(b) Matthew Maran; p16 Pascal Pittorino; front cover(tl) and p17 Andy
Rouse; p18(main) Tim Laman; p19 Doug Wechsler; p20 Bernard Castelein; front cover(tr) and p21
Alex Hyde; p22 Cyril Ruoso; p23 and p31(t) Jabruson; p24 Jabruson; p25 Pete Oxford; contents(b)
and p26 Aflo; p27 Pete Oxford; p28 Suzi Eszterhas; p29 Ian Lockwood.

Photographs supplied by Shutterstock: p9(inset) Hashim Pudiyapura;
Photographs supplied by Wikimedia: p18(inset) Bcameron54.

Every attempt has been made to clear copyright. Should there be any
inadvertent omission, please apply to the publisher for rectification.

The website addresses (URLs) included in this book were valid at the time
of going to press. However, it is possible that contents or addresses may
have changed since the publication of this book. No responsibility for any
such changes can be accepted by either the author or the Publisher.

CONTENTS

WHAT ARE FORESTS?

Forest biomes are areas with large numbers of trees covering the land. Trees are the giants of the plant kingdom.

In any forest, a smaller wood or even a small copse, trees dominate all other plants there. The trunk of this giant sequoia towers above the other trees in Kings Canyon National Park, California, USA.

Trees in all shapes and sizes

Trees grow in forests worldwide, but only in places with enough rainfall so their roots can suck up enough water to survive. They range from enormous redwoods and sequoias, which are the biggest living things on Earth, down to slender birch trees. They can have tiny leaves shaped like needles, or giant, flat leaves. But, however different, they have two things in common. They all have big, tough, woody stems that support them and they can live for many years.

Amazing Adaptation

Adaptations are special features or body parts that living things develop over time to help them survive in a biome. Trees get energy for growing so big from food. Like other green plants, they are adapted for making their own food by photosynthesis. Inside tree leaves, energy from sunlight is used to turn carbon dioxide gas from the air, and water sucked up through its roots, into sugary food.

Forest life

Forests are not just about trees. A whole host of living things are adapted to life in the forest biome. Plants, such as ferns and orchids, grow on the branches, and fungi grow on the forest floor. Animals, such as insects and monkeys, eat tree leaves and fruit, while others, including wild boar and deer, eat fallen nuts. Many predators, such as jaguars and chameleons, survive by catching forest prey.

Vital resource

During photosynthesis, plants release oxygen. Nearly all living things on Earth need oxygen to survive, as it is used to release energy from food in a process called respiration. Two-thirds of the total leaf area of all land plants in the world is found in forests, so forests are essential oxygen factories supporting life on our planet.

Chameleons are lizards that use branch-gripping feet to move through forests and long tongues to catch insect prey they have spotted with their swivelling eyes.

Fact Focus: Biome or Habitat?

Biomes are regions of the world that have a similar climate, plants and animals adapted to live there. Forests, deserts, grasslands, rivers, oceans and tundra are all biomes. A biome may be made of several habitats. A habitat is the specific place in a biome where a plant or animal lives, such as a particular type of tree or the depths of the ocean.

TYPES OF FORESTS

Forests can be divided up into four main types: taiga, deciduous, temperate rainforest and tropical rainforest. Each is distinct in character and the types of trees it contains.

Taiga

The taiga is forest found in the coldest parts of the Earth, where there is just enough water in the soil, which is not frozen, for trees to survive. Taiga has mostly coniferous trees, such as pine, spruce and fir, which make seeds in cones. These trees have leaves all year round and grow close together, so the biome is always dark.

Deciduous forest

Deciduous trees, including oak, beech, maple and chestnut, have leaves that change colour and fall to the ground in autumn. The trees remain bare through dark winters, surviving on stored food in their trunks. Then in spring new leaves appear and begin to make food.

Amazing Adaptation

Many coniferous trees have needle leaves (see page 10). They have a small surface area so they do not lose much water by evaporation. Holding onto water is important for trees when there is limited water in the soil. Needles also have a wax layer on the surface that protects them from cold and snow.

In a deciduous forest, leaves turn brown, yellow and red as they lose chlorophyll, the chemical that gives leaves their green colour and carries out photosynthesis.

Rainforest

Some forests grow in places where there is 2–6 metres of rainfall each year. This abundant moisture allows trees to grow very tall. Most of the tallest rainforest trees form a continuous canopy, or roof, over the forest. These plants get the most light.

Beneath the canopy, smaller trees and other plants, such as shrubs, survive using the light that filters through from above. The damp branches of trees are covered in epiphytes, plants, including mosses, orchids and ferns, that grow on others. Vines reach the light by twisting upwards around the trunks.

Tropical or temperate?

There are two types of rainforest. Tropical rainforest grows in places that are hot all year round and are very humid as water on the ground evaporates. Typical trees include figs, mahogany, kapok and eucalyptuses. Temperate rainforest grows in cooler places and typical trees include cedars, redwoods and cypresses.

In tropical rainforests, some tall trees, such as this fan palm, grow wide surface roots at ground level. These buttress roots act like stabilisers to support the trees' great height.

FORESTS AROUND THE WORLD

Forests cover around one third of all land on Earth. This biome is found worldwide except for the Poles and mountaintops, which are too cold for trees to grow, and desert areas, which are too dry and often too hot.

Moderate climate

Deciduous forest grows in western and central Europe, northeast Asia and eastern North America. Here the climate is temperate, which means not too cold but not too hot, with rain (and snow) spread through the year. The fallen leaves break down, or decompose, into nutrients that make the soil rich. All year round, there are gaps in the canopy that let light in. Nutrients and light help many plants grow on the forest floor.

Moderate and wet

The biggest area of temperate rainforest is along the west coast of North America, where the temperate climate is made wetter by rain and mist driving in off the Pacific Ocean. Temperate rainforest is also found in damp parts of South America, Japan, New Zealand and the UK.

Mosses grow on the trunks of these trees in a temperate rainforest in Washington, USA.

Northern forest

The taiga covers more land than other forest types. It is found in a broad swathe from North America across Northern Europe into Russia. There are two main seasons in the taiga: a short, warm and wet summer when trees do most of their growing, and a long, cold and dry winter. The taiga floor is dark and also low in nutrients, so not much grows beneath the trees.

The tropics

Most rainforest grows in tropical places. The tropics are areas north and south of the Equator, a line of equal distance between the Poles around the Earth. Here there is lots of rain, year-round warm temperatures, averaging 20–25°C and there is never frost or snow. With perfect growth conditions, it's no surprise that there can be 100 types of trees in every square kilometre.

Rainforests create their own rain, too. Water evaporates from the trees and condenses in the atmosphere to form clouds.

Amazing Adaptation

Tropical rainforest leaves often have drip tips to make rain pour off quickly during downpours. Then fungi and bacteria cannot grow on the surface in the humid conditions.

Arctic Ocean

North America
Europe
Asia

Atlantic Ocean
Africa

Pacific Ocean
South America

Indian Ocean
Pacific Ocean

Australia

- ■ Taiga
- ■ Deciduous forest
- ■ Tropical rainforest
- ■ Temperate rainforest

Antarctica

The map shows where the main taiga, deciduous forest, tropical rainforest and temperate rainforest areas are located around the world.

9

TAIGA LIFE

The taiga forests are home to a wide range of animals that have different ways of dealing with the varying seasons and surviving in the biome.

Seasonal foods

In the short taiga summer, leaf-eating animals, from caterpillars to deer, tuck into new, tender leaves on the taiga trees. Insects, such as butterflies, flies, moths and wood ants, are active, and usually have their young in this warmest taiga season.

The taiga becomes quieter in the harsh cold of winter. Many insects die but their young may survive over winter, hidden under bark on trees. Some insect-eating birds, like tits, move to warmer places further south, but other birds stay put. Crossbills have a year-round food supply because they eat the oil-rich seeds in the cones of coniferous trees.

The tips of each half of a crossbill's beak cross over the other. It twists the lower half away from the top half to open the scales on a cone. The crossbill sticks its tongue into the gap to pull out the seed inside.

Taiga residents

Some animals stay in the taiga all year round. Small plant-eating or herbivore mammals include snowshoe hares, squirrels and voles. They survive the cold using different adaptations. For example, squirrels stay warm by sleeping in protective drays (nests).

Larger herbivores include deer and moose, which are giant animals with broad antlers. Moose angle their heads back when running through dense vegetation. By doing this, the moose flattens its antlers so they don't snag on bushes and trees, allowing them to run faster to escape predators.

The taiga herbivores face the threat of predators as well as the cold. Taiga predators range from wild cats and pine martens, to wolves. A moose can weigh ten times as much as a wolf, but a pack of wolves can attack and kill it by working together.

Amazing Adaptation

Large herbivores, such as moose, have a smaller surface area relative to their volume, so they lose heat more slowly than smaller animals, in the cold, long winters of the taiga.

Moose eat leaves of broadleaved taiga trees, such as birch, mosses on tree branches and grasses in forest clearings.

TROPICAL RAINFOREST

There is a remarkable richness of life in tropical rainforests. This forest biome covers just six per cent of the Earth's land yet has over half of all known species of animals and plants!

Life in the trees

Many animals are perfectly adapted to live their whole lives in the canopy. For example, tree frogs have sucker-shaped fingertips to grip onto bark and leaves. Sloths slowly move through the branches hanging upside down from long, curved claws, grazing on leaves. Many monkeys and apes travel through the canopy in search of food, such as fruit and leaves. Gibbons swing along from branch to branch using massively powerful arms and shoulders.

The spider monkey's tail tip can curl around and grip branches. Hanging from its tail like a rope, the monkey can concentrate or selecting and plucking the freshest leaves.

Fact File: Salonga National Park

Location: Democratic Republic of Congo
Size: 36,000 km^2
Overview: The largest tropical rainforest reserve in Africa, protecting unspoilt and undeveloped forest, and home to rare animals including secretive forest elephants.

Insect universe

The range of types of living things in a biome, or particular place, is called biodiversity. Tropical rainforests have an enormous biodiversity of insect life. These rainforests are home to 80 per cent of all known insect species on our planet! They include giants of the insect world, such as 30-cm-long stick insects, and butterflies the width of a dinner plate. There are remarkable insect predators, such as praying mantises, which have giant clawed arms that shoot forward to spear victims.

A trip into this forest can be uncomfortable owing to the sheer abundance of insects, including swarms of blood-sucking flies, such as mosquitoes, and irritating sweat bees that land on people to drink the sweat off their skin! On the forest floor and all over the trees there are legions of ants, such as leafcutter and army ants, in search of food. Many live and move around in giant groups or colonies.

Leafcutter ants cut out pieces of leaf with their jaws and then carry them back to the nest balanced on their heads!

Amazing Adaptation

In the dark, humid interior of a leafcutter ant nest, the colony has a fungi garden, which it keeps supplied with leaves. Leaves are impossible for the ants to digest, but the fungi can decompose the leaves into sugars, which are eaten by the ants.

TEMPERATE RAINFOREST

The damp, misty, cool world of temperate rainforests is dominated by trees, such as redwoods and sequoias. These can grow more than 100 m tall and weigh hundreds of tonnes.

The forest floor

The giant trees of the temperate rainforest can live for thousands of years, but when they die, they leave a big hole in the canopy. New trees and other plants, such as sorrel and laurel, can grow in the patches of sunlight on the rich soil formed from decomposing trunks and leaves. The sodden, mossy soil is home to animals, including slugs and salamanders. Salamanders wriggle on short legs through the mosses hunting worms and ants, usually at night.

Amazing Adaptation

When threatened, an Ensatina salamander stands stiff-legged on its toes, arches its back down, and flips its tail towards the attacker. This shows off the bright underside of its tail, which has many glands that secrete sticky, milky poison.

The Ensatina salamander of western USA has a brown upper skin for camouflage on the forest floor, but an orange underside to warn predators, such as snakes, about its poisonous skin.

Bears in the forest

Temperate rainforests are often home to grizzly, brown and black bears. Black bears are the smallest of the three and are at most two metres long and weigh 270 kilogrammes. Black bears are the most common bear found in temperate rainforest. They use their long, tough claws for climbing and for digging into rotten trunks to unearth beetle larvae to eat, or to rip open bees' nests to get at the honey inside.

Black bears have a heavy coat of thick hair that not only keeps them warm in cool winters, but also dry in the damp forest air. During winter, there is less food in the forest. That's why black bears fatten up during summer when food, including shrub berries, is abundant.

Black bears can climb fast and high up trees, in search of eggs to eat in bird nests, to hide from predators, such as coyotes, or to reach a quiet spot to sleep.

Fact File: Fiordland National Park

Location: New Zealand
Size: 12,500 km²
Overview: The largest national park in New Zealand protects temperate rainforest of southern beech trees, along with flightless birds including kiwi and kakapo, a type of parrot.

DECIDUOUS FOREST LIFE

Deciduous forests provide shelter and food for a wide range of animals. Some, such as bumble bees and hoverflies, feed on the nectar of flowers that bloom before the new leaves emerge in spring.

Tree food

Deciduous trees provide food for many animals through the seasons. Some insects, such as moth caterpillars, nibble on leaves.

Others, such as cicadas, pierce the tree to drink fluid, called sap, flowing through tubes inside. Deer scrape off and eat bark, while squirrels feed on and store nuts to last the winter. Wild boar and badgers snuffle through the leaf litter in search of fallen nuts, insects, fungi and any other food they might come across.

Amazing Adaptation

Young cicadas burrow up to 2.5 m underground and feed on sap in tree roots. Some types remain here for up to 17 years avoiding predators, before burrowing out, climbing trees and changing into adults. Then predators, such as wasps, with much shorter life cycles will have forgotten cicadas were ever there!

Mouth

Cicadas have a short, sharp mouth shaped like a tube to pierce thick bark and wood to reach sap inside the tree.

Stripes and spots

Stripes and spots are patterns used as camouflage by different deciduous forest animals. This colouration is an adaptation for blending in with the fallen deciduous leaves, patches of dappled shade under the canopy, and even areas of tall grasses in clearings. For example, fallow deer have spots on their backs, wild boars have horizontal stripes and tigers have vertical black stripes on orange and white. When tigers are difficult to spot, they can get close to and pounce upon unsuspecting prey. This is helped by soft pads on the tiger's large paws, which help it to walk almost silently over dry leaves on the forest floor.

Tigers live in temperate, deciduous forests in India and Nepal.

Fact File: Chitwan National Park

Location: Nepal
Size: 932 km²
Overview: A reserve and World Heritage Site with a wide variety of forest plants, including bamboo and deciduous sal trees. This reserve is home to Bengal tigers and the one-horned rhinoceros.

FOREST LIFE CYCLES

The forest biome is the scene for some amazing and varied life cycles. A life cycle is the journey from egg to adult animal, or seed to adult plant.

Locked up!

When a female hornbill is ready to lay eggs, she climbs into a nest space inside a hollow tree and uses mud and poo to close up the hole, leaving just a tiny slit. The mud dries hard so she is locked in! She lays her eggs and waits until the young hatch, grow and develop feathers to fly before breaking out. She relies on her male mate to bring food for her and her young. This behaviour keeps out predators, such as snakes and other hornbills, that might kill the young when they are tiny.

The female hornbill stays imprisoned inside the tree until her hatched chicks grow too big for the space. Then she breaks them out!

Amazing Adaptation

Tree frogs live in the canopy far from ponds where they could lay eggs. Some solve this problem by laying their eggs in pools of water collected in epiphyte plants on branches in the canopy. The tadpoles eat insects that fall in this watery habitat or other eggs their mother lays there specially as food.

Ichneumon wasp

The female ichneumon wasp hovers over a tree trunk flicking her antennae. She feels vibrations from her prey: a larva munching through the wood inside. Then she injects an egg into the larva she has located. Her egg hatches into a wasp larva that eats the prey from the inside. Once fattened up over winter, the wasp larva transforms into an adult ichneumon wasp that burrows out of the wood.

The ichneumon raises her back end and drills a long, sharp tube through the wood to inject an egg into her prey hidden beneath the surface.

Brazil nut trees

Brazil nut tree seeds (brazil nuts) thud to the ground in very strong seed pods the size of grapefruits. Agoutis are rat-like mammals with big, chisel-shaped teeth tough enough to bite into the pod. They eat some nuts on the spot but also stuff their cheeks with others and carry them off to bury elsewhere in the forest for a future snack. With luck, a forgotten nut will germinate and have more space and sunlight to grow than under the canopy tree it fell from.

FOREST FOOD CHAINS

When a forest animal eats a plant or another animal, some of that energy passes to them. A food chain shows who eats who and therefore, who receives the energy.

The links in a chain

Any living thing needs energy to survive. The major source of energy in all biomes is sunlight. In the forest biome it is mostly trees that convert this into food by photosynthesis.

The next link in the chain is the herbivores, which take in some of that energy in the leaves, fruit, bark, roots and nuts they eat.

Then the animal-eaters or carnivores get in on the action, eating herbivores and other carnivores. For example, in Madagascan forests, lemurs eat tree leaves and fruit, and cat-like fossas eat lemurs.

Amazing Adaptation

The fossa hunts lemurs and other fast-moving prey in its forest food chain. It uses retractable claws to grip tree bark and a long tail as a counterbalance. Then the fossa doesn't fall during high-speed chases of prey through the canopy.

Fact Focus: Food Webs

Food webs show the diversity of feeding relationships in a place. They include many individual food chains together, often with overlapping links. For example, elephants, chimpanzees, monkeys and deer may all eat the same type of forest tree fruit when it is in season.

Final links

The fallen leaves, branches, dead animals, animal poo and other waste on the forest floor are an energy source for the final links in the forest food chain. These are scavengers, such as slugs, snails, millipedes and worms, and decomposers, including fungi and bacteria. Decomposers gain energy as they feed but also release nutrients into the soil that trees and other plants can use to grow.

Not all forest soils are rich in nutrients. Surprisingly, tropical rainforest soils are thin and low in nutrients. Dead matter, such as leaves, that falls from the trees decomposes rapidly in the humid conditions. But the tree roots grow in a mat over the soil and absorb the nutrients before they can get deep into the soil.

These extraordinary cup-shaped mushrooms are part of the fungi that has invaded and is speeding the decomposition of a fallen tree in a forest biome.

PEOPLE IN THE FOREST

Forest biomes are places where many people live. They can get most or all of the things they need to survive from forests, from animals they hunt, to materials for shelter and goods to sell.

Indigenous people

There are many distinct groups of indigenous people with particular beliefs, languages and identities living in particular parts of the forest biome worldwide. For example, in the Amazon tropical rainforest alone there are around one million people spread across some 400 tribes. Indigenous people living in the taiga include the Native American Cree people of Canada and Yakut people of Russia.

Baka tribe

Baka people of Central Africa are traditionally hunter-gatherers. Some hunt game, such as deer, using spears and bows and arrows, and make temporary camps in the forest as they move around. Many Baka people live in permanent villages. There they farm crops that they trade along with forest foods like honey, and products, such as baskets made from plant fibres.

A Baka mother and her child shelter in a temporary hut made from sticks and ngongo leaves in a tropical rainforest in Cameroon, Central Africa.

Changing population

Human populations in forests are changing. Foresters, farmers and miners are some of the people who come to live and work in the forest biome each year. New, larger settlements grow as places where these incomers can move to, shop and trade. Many forests receive lots of temporary visitors each year, too.

Forest tourism

Some tourists visit forests to get close to the remarkable biodiversity in its natural habitats, rather than in zoos or wildlife parks. For example, in some rainforests there are high wire walkways that lead visitors into the canopy. Other tourists hike or mountain bike along forest trails.

New roads with hard surfaces are built to take workers and tourists into the forest and move forest products out more easily without getting stuck in the mud!

FOREST RESOURCES

Forests are vast reserves of important resources that people need and want, such as wood and water.

Wood

The most obvious tree resource is wood which can be used to make a variety of timber products. Hardwoods, such as sapele or beech, are cut into planks to make furniture and sometimes musical instruments, but also sliced and glued together to make plywood used for construction. Wood from coniferous trees, called softwoods, are also widely used to make buildings and also ground up into wood pulp, to make paper and the absorbent filling of nappies!

Fact Focus: Fuelwood

Globally around 2.5 billion people, or over a third of Earth's total population, rely on fuelwood, often foraged from forests, to burn for cooking food. Some use mostly charcoal, a black fuel made by carefully heating and drying wood of different types.

This African hardwood tree has been cut down by loggers with powerful chainsaws to be used for timb

Non-timber resources

Forest plants provide many resources beyond timber. These include fruit, nuts, bark and leaves, which can be used as foods, raw materials, or even ingredients in a broad range of medicines. Rainforest flowers are the basis for some important cancer treatments.

Forests also mask hidden resources. The soil revealed by clearing forests can be used for farming. For example, tropical rainforests are cleared to raise cattle, and grow food crops, such as soya beans and oil palm. Land under some forests is a store of valuable and useful minerals. For example, beneath the taiga are supplies of coal, oil, iron, silver, gold and diamonds.

Water supplies

Forests create and clean water supplies. Roots hold the soil together, preventing soil washing into and dirtying water supplies, and this stable soil along with leaf litter soaks up rainwater in the forest floor. The soil filters the water and gradually releases it into streams, rivers and groundwater supplies. Forests also prevent flooding on land by storing water after heavy downpours.

This forester in Guyana, South America, is cutting into a tree bark so latex oozes from the grooves and collects in a container. The latex is used to make natural rubber.

FOREST THREATS

Deforestation is the biggest threat to forests, and it is increasing as the global population grows. At present an area of about 48 football fields of forest is lost every minute.

Out of control

Logging is cutting and removing whole trees from forests. It is controlled in some places, but mostly happens illegally, even in protected forests, such is the demand for rare and valuable hardwoods. People also clear forest, especially to farm or mine under it, by burning. Fires can rapidly get out of control, especially if peat soil beneath sets alight.

Fact Focus: Global Warming

Global warming is the rise in Earth's average temperature, caused by heat being trapped in the atmosphere by greenhouse gases, such as carbon dioxide.

Deforestation makes global warming worse. First, there are fewer trees so there is less photosynthesis and less carbon dioxide being removed from the atmosphere. Second, burning waste wood produces more carbon dioxide. Third, bacteria in peat soils release lots of methane gas. Methane stores more heat than carbon dioxide.

A rainforest in Brazil burns in order to clear the land ready for farming. Forest fires cause immense danger to forest life and humans, not only from spreading fire, but also from choking smoke.

Deep impacts

Deforestation has deep impacts on forest life. Animals are killed directly in forest fires and by loggers. Roads, settlements and farmland can break up areas of forest into smaller, isolated patches. In such fragmented habitats animals may not be able to find enough food or meet other animals to breed with. Roads allow better access into the remaining forest not only for legal activities, but also for illegal hunting and logging.

Foresters sometimes create plantations on cleared land, but these new forests have few tree species and are treated with chemicals, so they cannot support biodiversity like natural forests. And farmland where tropical rainforest once stood often cannot grow crops for long, because the soil is low in nutrients, so farmers abandon this land and cut down more forest.

This soldier in Central Africa has confiscated illegally hunted forest deer called duiker to prevent poachers making money from hunting and selling this bushmeat.

Fact Focus: Natural Threats

Natural deforestation can occur after natural disasters, such as volcanic eruptions and forest fires started by lightning strikes. It can also occur when insects invade and kill trees. For example, emerald ash borer beetles kill ash trees by feeding under the bark, which stops the flow of water and sap.

FOREST FUTURES

Forests are an astonishing and critically important biome for all inhabitants of our planet. This is the reason why people are working to protect them now and for the future.

In this forest reserve in Borneo, Indonesia, an orphan orangutan whose mother was killed by loggers is being helped to explore the biome and find food. The hope is that in future it will be able to live and look after itself in the rainforest.

Reserves

Only around ten per cent of global forest is protected, which is about half the area of the United States. Governments and charities fence off areas of forest and employ rangers to watch out for hunters and illegal logging. Usually there are few rangers for a large area, so people use satellites to help spot illegal activities from space. Most conservation efforts are directed at forests with high conservation value because they have unusual or well-known species, such as orangutans, or rich biodiversity.

Fact File: Olympic Forest Reserve

Location: Brazil
Size: 1 km²
Overview: This reserve protects a small section of the biodiverse Atlantic Forest in Brazil. It was funded by a public appeal for donations during the Olympic Games in Rio in 2016. The reserve protects endangered animals, including woolly spider monkeys and crowned eagles.

Changing habits

People are protecting forest by making sure they buy wood or timber products only from legally logged forests that are sustainable. Sustainable forestry means logging some trees, not the oldest and rarest sorts, and replanting with young trees of similar species to retain forest cover and biodiversity. Others are establishing new forests by planting new trees.

In many forests, scientists are working to study forest life in order to better understand the impacts of deforestation and future impacts on forests of further global warming. Their knowledge and advice can help us change our habits to protect this planet's forest future.

Time to recreate lost forest! These women in Bangladesh are helping to plant rubber trees to create new forest.

GLOSSARY

adaptation special feature or behaviour that helps a living thing survive.

bacteria tiny living things that can cause diseases or decompose waste.

biodiversity variety of life or range of living things in a place

biome large region of Earth with living things adapted to the typical climate, soils and other features.

camouflage colour, pattern or shape that makes it hard to identify an object against the background it is in.

canopy main leafy layer of a forest

carnivore meat-eating animal

climate typical weather pattern through the year in an area

colony group of individuals living together.

coniferous tree that makes seeds in cones.

counterbalance weight balancing another weight.

deciduous trees with leaves that fall as a response to a drop in temperature.

decompose break down into simpler pieces.

decomposer living things that break down bits of dead plants, animals and waste.

deforestation destruction and removal of forest

epiphyte plant that grows on another, larger plant.

evaporation change of state from liquid to gas

filter remove pieces from a liquid.

food chain way of showing what animals eats what in a chain.

food web feeding relationships between living things, usually in a particular habitat or biome

fragmented broken up into smaller, unconnected pieces.

fuelwood wood used primarily to burn for cooking or warming homes.

fungi type of living thing, such as mushrooms or yeasts, that mostly decompose living things after they die and their waste.

germinate when a young plant emerges from a seed.

global warming rise in average temperature of Earth caused by human activity.

greenhouse gas gas, such as carbon dioxide, that traps heat from the Sun in the atmosphere.

habitat place where an animal or plant typically lives.

herbivore plant-eating animal

indigenous people who have lived in a place for a very long time and have strong historical, cultural and other associations with it.

larva young stage of insects and other animals

leaf litter part of forest soil made from decomposing dead leaves releasing nutrients.

logging felling and removing trees.

minerals naturally occurring chemicals, such as iron and coal

mucus slime produced by living things.

natural resources things found in nature that are useful to people.

nectar sweet liquid made in flowers to attract animals which help plants make seeds.

nutrient chemical substances essential for living things to be healthy, grow and live.

peat soil made from partly decomposed plants, which is often boggy.

photosynthesis process by which green plants make sugary food using sunlight.

predator animal that hunts and eats others.

prey animals hunted and eaten by others.

ranger person who helps to protect a place.

reserve area protected to keep living things and landscapes of special interest safe from people.

sap fluid transported inside a plant.

scavenger animal that feeds on dead animals, plants or waste.

sustainable carried out without damaging natural resources.

FIND OUT MORE

Books
Rainforests (Research on the Edge)
Louise Spilsbury
Wayland, 2015

What Happens if the Rainforests Disappear? (Unstable Earth)
Mary Colson
Wayland, 2014

Tropical Rainforests (Amazing Habitats)
Tim Harris
Franklin Watts, 2017

Wildfires
Seymour Simon
Collins, 2016

Websites
Check out more facts about the biome at:

http://www.ucmp.berkeley.edu/exhibits/biomes/forests.php

Compare the contrasting world biomes at:

http://kids.nceas.ucsb.edu/biomes/index.html

Discover all you need to know about tropical rainforests at:

http://kids.mongabay.com/

including details about its structure at:

http://kids.mongabay.com/elementary/004.html

Webcam:

http://www.worldlandtrust.org/webcams/ornithos1

INDEX